Praise for
The Fix-It Friends: Have No Fear!

"Fears are scary! But don't worry: the Fix-It Friends know how to vanquish all kinds of fears, with humor and step-by-step help. Nicole C. Kear has written a funny and helpful series."

—Fran Manushkin, author of the Katie Woo series

"Full of heart and more than a little spunk, this book teaches kids that fear stands no chance against friendship and courage. Where were the Fix-It Friends when I was seven years old?"

—Kathleen Lane, author of *The Best Worst Thing*

"I love the Fix-It Friends as a resource to give to the families I work with. The books help kids see their own power to overcome challenges—and they're just plain fun to read."

—Lauren Knickerbocker, PhD, Co-Director, Early Childhood Clinical Service, NYU Child Study Center

"Hooray for these young friends who work together; this diverse crew will have readers looking forward to more."

—*Kirkus Reviews*

The Fix-It Friends

Three's a Crowd

Nicole C. Kear
illustrated by Tracy Dockray

[Imprint]
MAKE YOUR MARK

NEW YORK

[Imprint]

MAKE YOUR MARK

A part of Macmillan Publishing Group, LLC
175 Fifth Avenue, New York, NY 10010

THE FIX-IT FRIENDS: THREE'S A CROWD. Text copyright © 2018 by Nicole C. Kear.
Illustrations copyright © 2018 by Imprint. All rights reserved.
Printed in the United States of America by
LSC Communications, Harrisonburg, Virginia.

Library of Congress Control Number: 2017945051

Our books may be purchased in bulk for promotional,
educational, or business use. Please contact your local
bookseller or the Macmillan Corporate and Premium Sales
Department at (800) 221-7945 ext. 5442 or by e-mail at
MacmillanSpecialMarkets@macmillan.com.

Book design by Ellen Duda
Illustrations by Tracy Dockray
Imprint logo designed by Amanda Spielman

First edition, 2018

ISBN 978-1-250-11581-2 (hardcover)

1 3 5 7 9 10 8 6 4 2

ISBN 978-1-250-08674-7 (trade paperback)

1 3 5 7 9 10 8 6 4 2

ISBN 978-1-250-08675-4 (ebook)

mackids.com

Hello! I'm Cora, and I'm very pleased to meet you.
Stealing books is not just against the law; it's very impolite. I've never stolen
a book. I've never even stolen a look! But I think really awful things could
happen to you if you do it. You might even lose your best friend.

For Nonny,

Con tutto il cuore

With special thanks to expert consultant

Randi Pochtar, PhD, of the NYU Child Study Center

I'm Veronica Conti, and I'm a happy-endings kind of person.

If I see a cloud, I look for the silver lining.

If life gives me lemons, I make delicious lemonade, sell it in front of my house, and make a bunch of money.

And if I ask my mom if we can go to the trampoline gym for my eighth birthday and she says "We'll see," I know that what she really means is "You betcha!"

"Oh, thank you, thank you!" I exclaimed when my mom said "We'll see."

"You really are an optimist," said my mom, smiling.

"Mom, I'm not even eight yet!" I said. "I'm too young to be a doctor!"

"That's an *optometrist*," said my big brother, Jude. He is in fourth grade, so he thinks he knows

everything. "An *optimist* is just a positive person. You know—someone who thinks most endings will be happy ones."

"That's me for sure!" I chirped.

It was true. I did think all endings would be happy. And when it looked like a story wouldn't have a happy ending because there was a problem, then I'd just fix the problem! And if I didn't know how to fix it, then I'd ask Jude or his best friend, Ezra, or my best friend, Cora. We were the Fix-It Friends!

Until something broke that seemed too hard to fix.

It all started in the beginning of March. With Margot.

Chapter 2

March has always been my favorite month.

I know March is not as popular as the "-ember" months with all their great holidays, but don't be duped! March is the super supreme best! Here's why:

1. It's the start of spring! Which means it gets sunny, and you don't need to wear heavy, itchy jackets anymore, and the flowers start to bloom, and the baby birds hatch.

2. When you get to March, you know that the school year is more than

half over, which is another way of saying, "Summer vacation, here we come!"

3. Last but not least . . . my birthday is in March!

I wanted my eighth birthday party to be the best ever. Cora and I brainstormed a ton of ideas. She has been helping me plan my parties since we became best friends in kindergarten. Cora is a big help because she is organized and responsible and loves holding a clipboard.

Our first idea was to rent a horse to give rides to all our friends. I wanted a black stallion or a white stallion, but really I'd have settled for a donkey or even a Great Dane. But Dad said we couldn't ride a stallion down city streets. Also, it costs too much.

Cora had the great idea to do a pet spa in the living room. But the only pet I have is a goldfish, and Mom said we could not dye Fred's scales or put bubble bath in his tank. So that idea was out.

Then, in the beginning of March, when I was eating breakfast before school, I saw an ad in the newspaper:

Think you need wings to fly? Think again!
All you need is your two legs and our
MEGA JUMBO TURBO TRAMPOLINE!
Announcing the grand opening of
The House of Bounce,
where the sky really is the limit!

30% off all admissions in March!
Ask about our class trips and party packages!

"Eureka!" I shouted.

I showed Mom the ad. She had not had her coffee yet and I was sure she was going to say "Forget it," but instead she said "We'll see." And, as all optimists know, that just means "Sure thing, sweet pea!"

That's when my little sister, Pearl, ran into the kitchen. She was sucking on her paci and holding the waist of her pajama pants so they wouldn't fall down. Pearl's big diaper used to hold up her pants, but since she got potty trained and stopped wearing diapers, her pants are always falling down to her ankles.

Pearl must have heard us talking about birthdays because she popped her pacifier out of her mouth and yelled, "Bifday? Yay! Is my BIFDAY!"

She jumped up and her pants dropped down.

"No, honey, not yet. We're talking about Veronica's birthday, which is at the end of this month," said Mom, pulling Pearl's pants up.

"I wanna bifday!" Pearl whined. Then she pouted.

My dad calls this Pearl's Power Pout because it packs a punch. Her bottom lip sticks out so far that it looks like a window ledge. Her big blue eyes get enormous and all wet and shiny. She looks sadder than a really hungry golden retriever waiting for you to throw her a scrap of food from your dinner.

No one can refuse Pearl when she does her

Power Pout. But I couldn't change her birthday even if I wanted to.

"You'll be turning three next month, in April," I told her. "Your birthday is practically here."

Three's a Crowd

"Yay! My bifday!!" She clapped with glee and then told Mom very seriously, "I wanna wat!"

That's how Pearl says "rat." She talks about rats all the time because they are her all-time favorite animal. Both my grandma who lives in Texas and my grandma who lives upstairs think it's the creepiest thing ever. They both have tried to get her to like something more cute and cuddly, like kittens or ponies or butterflies. But it never works.

Pearl's best friend is a stuffed-animal rat named Ricardo. She got him for her second birthday and has dragged him around everywhere since then. At first, she dragged him by his tail. Then his tail fell off, and Dad had to duct-tape it back on. So she dragged him by his ear, and his ear fell off, so Dad duct-taped *that* on, too. Jude calls him "Franken-rat."

"Pearl, my girl, I know you and your sister want a furry pet," said Dad, lifting her into his arms, "but you know I'm allergic."

Pearl did not seem to hear him. She hugged Ricardo tight and said, "I wanna wat and cake! Wif butterfwy-miwk icing! And faiwy-dust spwinkles!"

Jude put down the book he was reading, *Revenge of the Swamp Zombies.* "Cake with butterfly-milk icing and fairy-dust sprinkles? That sounds really tasty. Can I come to your party?"

"Jude!" I protested. "Stop encouraging her."

But it was too late. Pearl was stomping around and singing, "My bifday! My bifday! Minemine-mineminemine!"

Chapter 3

I was so happy about having my party at the House of Bounce that I skipped into school that morning. I couldn't wait to tell Cora the good news.

"I found the perfect thing to do for my birthday party!" I told Cora as we hung our jackets on their hooks. "I'll give you a hint: It rhymes with drama queen."

"A movie screen?" asked Cora in her high-pitched chipmunk voice.

"Nope!"

"Magical Mystery Mini-Golf?"

"No, silly! That doesn't rhyme with drama queen."

"Hmmm . . . smarma-zine?"

"What? No! That's not even a word!" I giggled. "It's going to be on a *trampoline!*" I exclaimed. "At the House of Bounce!"

Cora jumped up and down in excitement, which made all her red curls bounce like crazy. Her flouncy blue dress ballooned out like a parachute.

When she was done jumping, we did our secret handshake. It's what we do when we are:

1. Excited.

2. Nervous.

3. Bored.

So, basically, anytime! We created it in kindergarten and just keep adding to it, so it has become a real masterpiece.

Here's how we do it:

Three's a Crowd

We ▮▮▮▮, then we ▮▮▮▮▮ ▮▮▮ ▮▮ ▮▮▮, and after that we ▮▮▮▮▮▮ ▮▮▮▮, but don't forget about the ▮▮▮▮▮ing, and finally, the best part of all, we ▮▮▮▮.

Ha! You didn't think I'd actually *tell* you! It's a secret!

"I can't wait for the party!" Cora said when we were done. Then she frowned. "Will Minnie be back in time?"

Minnie had just left for Puerto Rico with her moms to visit her grandma, who was sick. She didn't know when she'd be back.

"I hope so," I said, sliding into my seat across from Cora. "I miss her."

"Me too," said Cora. "Antarctica isn't the same without her."

No, Antarctica was not the land where we lived. It was just the name of our table at school. Miss Mabel named each of the tables after the seven continents. I loved being at Antarctica because it's the *coolest* continent. Ha!

Antarctica was already a small table to begin with, but with Minnie gone, it was just Cora and Wren and me. Wren is a very serious boy. He has black hair that reaches his shoulders and hangs down in front of his face. Wren has never said one mean word to me. He hasn't really said one nice word to me, either. Pretty much all he says is "yes" and "no" and "I don't know." Sometimes he says "no comment," which I always think is funny because it's exactly the same as not saying anything at all! It is impossible to tell how he's feeling and whether he likes something or hates it. He's basically the opposite of me.

I heard the pretty, chime-y sounds of a xylophone, which is what Miss Mabel plays to tell us it's time to settle down and listen up. It is such a relaxing way to start the day and just one of the reasons why she is my favorite teacher of all time.

"Good morning," said Miss Mabel. She looked marvelous in black pants with little white stripes and a black sweater that had a big zebra face on it.

"This morning, I have some really exciting news—"

Right away, everyone started guessing what it could be.

"You won the lottery!"

"No more homework?"

"You're taking us to Disneyland?"

That was my guess. It's always my guess, and it is always wrong.

Miss Mabel chimed the xylophone again to get everyone's attention. "The exciting news is that we'll be welcoming a new student tomorrow!"

I was so excited that I felt like a popcorn popper! Cora squealed with excitement, too. Wren didn't make a sound.

Miss Mabel wrote on the whiteboard:

MARGOT DUBOIS

"This is how you spell her name," Miss Mabel said. "If you'd like to write her a welcome card, I'll give you a few minutes to do that now. She's just moved here from California with her mom, and she likes . . ." Miss Mabel looked down at her note-pad. "She likes designing clothes, swimming, and playing with her bulldog, Bernie."

"She loves fashion design!" Cora said to me. Cora absolutely loves clothes. Especially dresses. Especially dresses loaded down with a zillion sequins.

"She has a bulldog!" I exclaimed.

"Your favorite breed!" said Cora.

A big, annoyed groan came from behind me, from the Asia table. I turned around and saw Matthew Sawyer sitting there, wiggling one of his top teeth that was really, really, really loose. He tried to tug the tooth out, but even though it was only hanging on by a thread, it wouldn't come loose, so he let go and wiped his gross, slobbery fingers on his striped shirt.

"Another dog lover," he complained. "How unoriginal. Everyone always has dogs! Like that's the *only* kind of pet a person can have! What about tarantulas? Or hissing cockroaches? What about fleas? With fleas, you can make a circus. I'd like to see a dog be in a circus! Am I right, Wren?"

Wren blinked and then said, "I don't know."

I was about to tell Matt "Of course dogs can be in the circus!" but then I thought he was probably kidding.

The thing about Matthew Sawyer is that when you think he's kidding, he's serious. And when you think he's serious, he's kidding. You can never tell with him!

So I just said, "I don't have time for Matthew Sawyer business right now. I have to make a card that will wow the new girl."

Three's a Crowd

"Why?" He scowled. "You already have a best friend."

"I'm not looking for a new best friend! I could never replace Cora!" I exclaimed very impatiently. "But a person can never have too many friends. Don't you think so, Wren?"

"Yes," Wren said.

"Absolutely!" chirped Cora.

Then Miss Mabel called Cora to her desk, and I got started on my welcome card. I wrote Margot's name on the front with my shimmery turquoise marker. Inside, I wrote a poem.

> Hello and welcome, dear Margot!
> What's your last name? I forgot.
> Here's a bit about me (okay, a lot!):
> I love chocolate that's steaming hot
> and peppermint tea from a pot.
> I use tissues when I've got snot,
> I don't eat apples with any rot,
> and I love to ride horses, *trot trot trot.*
> Is this poem crazy? I hope not!
> Well, good-bye for now, dear Margot!

Three's a Crowd

I showed it to Cora, who said, "She's going to love it. I'll put it on the top of the pile when I give her the cards after school."

"You're meeting her after school?" I asked.

"Miss Mabel asked me if I could show her around the school this afternoon," said Cora.

I felt really disappointed that Miss Mabel didn't pick me to be Margot's tour guide. Everyone knows I'm super friendly. I'm the president of the Fix-It Friends, for crying out loud. I'm a professional helper!

I was about to beg Cora to beg Miss Mabel to let me help, but then I remembered I had to go to gymnastics class anyway.

So I just sighed.

"Don't forget to tell her all about me!" I said.

Cora smiled. "How could I forget to tell her about my best friend in the whole world?"

Chapter 4

That night as soon as I got home from gymnastics, I called Cora. I tried her mom's phone four times, but it kept going right to voice mail. I knew it had run out of battery. This happens a lot. It's because Mrs. Klein gets really busy chasing after all her children and forgets to charge her phone.

Cora and her identical twin sister, Camille, don't really get into trouble, but they have little brothers who are wild and mischievous. Bo and Lou are also identical twins, and they are five years old. They are always climbing too high or trying to karate chop things that you shouldn't karate chop.

So Cora's mom is always busy with those boys, and her phone is usually out of battery. That's why I didn't get to talk to Cora that night after gymnastics class. I had to wait until the next morning.

I was so excited to hear about the new girl that I dragged Mom and Jude to school super early. The door of the school wasn't even unlocked yet, so Jude and I sat down to wait. I practiced my hand-stands while Jude read his book.

After a few minutes, I spotted Cora's family. Well, I didn't spot them so much as hear them.

"NINJA SPEED!" bellowed Bo . . . or was it Lou? Most days, I can't tell them apart because they have the same short, curly hairstyle and share all the same clothes.

They both ran as fast as they could through the gate and into the yard that leads to the doors of our school.

"NINJA POWER!" bellowed the other one, who could have been Lou or Bo. They did a whole bunch of roundhouse kicks.

"NINJA KNOCKOUT!" they screamed at the same time, punching the air and yelling "Yeah! Yeah! Yeah!"

Far behind Bo and Lou came Cora and Camille.

Cora and Camille are also identical, but it's easy to tell them apart. Sure, they have the same super-curly red hair, but Cora's is long—almost to her shoulders—and Camille's is cut short and always really messy. Cora is neat and tidy, and she almost always wears dresses or skirts. Usually her dresses have pleats or polka dots or poofy stuff underneath them.

Three's a Crowd

Camille only ever wears sweatpants or shorts and T-shirts. She absolutely loves playing basketball and has become really good at it. It seems like there is a magnet in her fingers and another magnet in the ball so that the ball always leaps right into her hands.

Behind all of them came Mrs. Klein, who was holding an enormous cup of coffee. She was

wearing purple plaid pajama pants and her jacket was buttoned up crooked.

"Hey, it's the Conti kids!" exclaimed Mrs. Klein. "How's tricks?"

One reason I love Mrs. Klein is because she doesn't talk in the same, boring way that most grown-ups talk. The other reason I love her is because she lets us watch TV and eat candy at her house.

"I'm good," said Jude. He looked up from his book but only for a second. Once he starts reading, he gets totally sucked in and it's like he's not even in the same room as you anymore.

"Never been better!" I told Mrs. Klein. "How are you?"

"Well, I'm in my jammies, I need about five more cups of joe before I'm really awake, and my house looks like a natural disaster hit it." She laughed loudly. "In other words: same old, same old."

Then Bo—or it could have been Lou—shrieked, and Mrs. Klein chased after the boys, yelling, "No, no, no! Bo, put that stick down this minute! Lou! What's that you got? Is that BROKEN GLASS?"

I turned to Cora and said, "So? What's the new girl like? Tall or short? Shy or friendly? What's her favorite color? What's her favorite ice-cream flavor? Does she have any allergies?"

Cora giggled. "Oh, I don't know any of that! I only talked to her for a little while. But guess what? Her mom's a fashion designer! So she has really cool outfits. And she said she could teach me how to sew!"

"That's so cool!" I said. "Hey, did you give her my card? Did she like it?"

"Yes, she did," said Cora. "Only her name is pronounced Mar-*go*, not Mar-*got*."

"But it has a *T* at the end of it!" I exclaimed.

"Yes, but it's silent."

A silent *T*! Whoever heard of such a thing?

"Oh no!" I moaned. "That means my whole card must have seemed so dumb!"

"It's okay," said Cora. "She liked it anyway."

Then the red double doors of the school opened, which meant we could go inside, so Cora and I did. Jude was still reading his book and didn't even notice.

"Earth to Jude!" I yelled over my shoulder. "Schooltime!"

Where would he be without me, I ask you?

Chapter 5

I was in the middle of unpacking my backpack when I heard Miss Mabel say, "Hello, Margot!" It rhymed.

I looked over at the door of our classroom and saw Margot Dubois. Here is what she looked like:

1. Bright orange hair. Margot's hair was the color of a carrot! But the color wasn't even the most unusual part about it. Her hair was very straight and cut so that it was way longer in the front than it was in the back.

The Fix-It Friends

I had never seen a haircut like that in all my life!

2. Green eyes that looked like emeralds!

3. Her clothes were covered in zippers. Her jacket had zippers up the sleeves, and the front of her shirt had a whole bunch of little zippers in the shape of a heart. Even her jeans had zippers going up the sides.

4. In her ears were two silver earrings. They were in the shape of letters. One ear had a G and the other ear had an O. *Go?* I thought to myself. *Go where?*

Miss Mabel walked Margot over to the hooks on the wall and showed her where to hang

Three's a Crowd

up her jacket and backpack. Then she walked Margot right over to my table!

"Margot, welcome to Antarctica," said Miss Mabel. "You already know Cora, and this is Veronica and Wren. They make a wonderful welcome committee."

Margot slipped into the empty seat next to Cora.

"You'll take good care of her, won't you, guys?" asked Miss Mabel.

"Absolutely!" I sang.

"Of course!" chirped Cora.

Wren nodded.

As soon as Miss Mabel walked away, I said to Margot, "Hello! Welcome! *¡Bienvenidos!* That's Spanish. My friend Minnie taught it to me. She sits at this table, too!"

"Is she invisible?" asked Margot.

"Ummm, no," I replied. "She's in Puerto Rico."

"I was just kidding," said Margot with a smile.

"Oh, right," I said. "Ha!" Then I didn't know what to do, so I laughed really, really hard. Cora giggled, too. Wren was silent.

"Cool earrings!" I said to Margot. "Are they sending a secret message?"

Margot scrunched her eyebrows together, like she was confused.

"Like, to go somewhere?" I asked. "Because they say 'Go'?"

"Ohhhhhh. No," she replied. "That's just my nickname. Gogo."

I felt like I was making a whole bunch of mistakes with Margot. The harder I tried, the more stuff I got wrong.

"I love your shirt," said Cora. "Did your mom design it?"

Margot nodded. "It's part of my mom's clothing line for kids. She just started it—that's why we moved here. The zippers were my idea. I love love love zippers. They add zing!"

"I love zing!" I chirped. "Don't you, Wren?"

"No comment," Wren said.

For the first time, I thought maybe I should be more like Wren. I felt like I had too many comments for my own good.

Chapter 6

Margot sat with Cora and me at lunch, so we got to know her.

We found out the things she loved:

1. Her bulldog, Bernie, who was two human years old.

2. Swimming and diving.

3. Zippers.

4. Saying words three times in a row, like, "It's so fun fun fun!" and "Cool cool cool!" and "Please please please!"

5. Disneyland, which she's been to loads

of times. She even had her eighth birthday there!

She was just telling us her secret for riding Space Mountain without waiting in a long line when I saw Miss Tibbs walking toward our table.

"Uh-oh. Miss Tibbs Alert!" I whispered. "She's pretty much the meanest recess and lunch teacher in the universe. One wrong move and you'll get the longest lecture of your life."

"Hello there," said Miss Tibbs. "Miss Conti, won't you introduce me to your new friend?"

"Sure," I said. "Miss Tibbs, this is Margot. Her name is spelled with a *T* at the end, but it's silent."

"It must be French," said Miss Tibbs.

"*Bien sûr,*" said Margot.

"*Parlez-vous français?*" Miss Tibbs asked Margot.

Then Margot said a whole bunch of stuff in

French that I did not understand at all. But it must have been funny, because Miss Tibbs threw her head back and laughed.

"*Oui oui*," said Miss Tibbs to Margot, still smiling.

I didn't know Miss Tibbs spoke French! And I've known Miss Tibbs for three years! Also, Miss Tibbs has never, ever laughed at any of my jokes, even though I am pretty famous for being one of the funniest second graders at our school.

When Miss Tibbs walked away, Margot said, "She doesn't seem mean at all! She seems really nice."

"Well, she's not usually like that," I said quickly. "She's in a really good mood today for some weird reason."

"You speak French so well!" said Cora.

Three's a Crowd

"Oh, thanks. My babysitter back home taught me," she said. Then she looked really sad all of a sudden. She cleared her school lunch tray and went to the bathroom.

Cora said, "Poor Margot. She's so homesick. We have to be really nice to her. We have to make sure she feels included."

"Okay," I said. The truth was that I wasn't so sure how I felt about Margot and I sort of liked things the way they were. But I knew Cora was right, so that week I invited Margot to do lots of stuff.

I invited her to my birthday party.

I invited her to sit with Cora and me at lunch.

I even invited her to play tag at recess with my tag gang—Noah, Camille, and Cora. After all, with Minnie away, we were missing a player.

The Fix-It Friends

Margot played tag with us every day that week. On Friday, she said, "Hey, do you guys want to play Blob Tag?"

"What's that?" Camille asked.

"Oh, it's the best best best! When the person who's 'It' tags you, you have to hold hands, and every time you tag someone, they join on the end

of everyone holding hands. You hold hands until you get everyone. It's awesome!"

I really wanted to play Air Tag because it's the only kind of tag where Noah doesn't win. Noah is the absolute fastest person on the ground, but in Air Tag your feet can't touch the ground, and that really slows him down.

I was about to tell Margot "No thanks," but everyone else was already saying "Yeah! Sure!" and nodding with excitement.

So we played Blob Tag.

Was it fun?

Sure.

But I still didn't like it. I didn't like it at all.

Chapter 7

I was starving after playing Blob Tag at recess, so I couldn't wait to gobble my lunch. Dad had packed me a salami sandwich, made just the way I like it, with four slices of salami and two slices of provolone cheese stuck in the middle of soft Italian bread.

"Deeee-lish!" I said.

Cora opened up her lunch box and sighed.

"Loco Lunch Box again?" I asked. She nodded.

"What's Loco Lunch Box?" asked Margot as she opened up the milk carton on her school lunch tray.

Three's a Crowd

"That's what we call it when my mom runs out of time in the morning to pack a lunch and just tosses weird stuff into my lunch box," Cora explained.

Cora showed us what was inside her lunch box:

1. A little packet of duck sauce.
2. Half of a cinnamon-raisin bagel.
3. A really big radish with the stem still on it.

"It's not the worst Loco Lunch Box," I said. "I bet we can fix it. Duck sauce might be good on a cinnamon-raisin bagel."

I can find the silver lining in any cloud.

But did Margot want to see the beautiful silver lining I found? No!

"Duck sauce on a bagel?" Margot grimaced.

"Okay, then, Cora, you can just take half of my sandwich," I offered. I always fix Cora's Loco Lunches. I'm a professional fixer, after all.

"Why don't you just get the school lunch?" asked Margot. "They have BBQ chicken today. It's pretty good."

Margot stabbed a piece of BBQ chicken with her fork and handed the fork to Cora.

"Oh, Cora won't like it," I explained to Margot. "She's very picky."

But while I was in the middle of talking, Cora stuck the bite in her mouth and said, "Not bad."

"What?" I asked.

"Right?" Margot asked.

"It's actually really good!" said Cora as she chewed. And, to my amazement, she walked over to the school lunch line and told the lunch lady her name so she could get a tray.

"But Cora hates school lunch," I said. I was talking to myself, but Margot answered me.

"People change their minds sometimes," she said.

"I guess," I said. But what I was really thinking was that Cora never changed her mind before Margot showed up. And I was worried, because there was no telling what Cora might change her mind about next.

Chapter 8

That Sunday, I invited Cora to come over so we could plan my birthday extravaganza. She said she couldn't because she had to go to swimming lessons.

"Since when do you take swimming lessons?" I asked her.

"Since today. It's my first one!"

I knew right away where she got the idea for those swimming lessons. After all, Margot loved loved loved swimming and talked about it all the time. I knew it was no big deal, but it just made me jealous.

Three's a Crowd

On Monday morning, before Margot got to school, I invited Cora to come over my house after school.

"You can help me make party hats for the guests!" I said. "We can put sequins on them, if you want."

Sequins are Cora's weakness. If something involves sequins, she can't say no!

But she did exactly that.

"Oooooh, that sounds fun, but I can't," she replied. "Margot's mom invited me to visit her studio. She wants to thank me for showing Margot around. She's going to teach me how to sew!"

I suddenly felt really angry.

"But you didn't even help her that much!" I protested. "And I've helped her with tons of stuff!"

Cora's big brown eyes got wide with surprise. Then she looked down. I felt bad that I had made her sad. I wanted to apologize and do our secret handshake. But then I thought about how Cora was going to a real fashion studio and didn't even invite me, and I was too mad to be nice.

"It doesn't matter," I said really quickly, "because I just remembered that I have to . . ." I tried to think of an exciting activity. "I have to meet with Ezra . . . to finish recording my demo album."

"Cool," said Cora.

"Cool," I said back.

At recess, I did not ask Margot if she wanted to play tag with us, but she did anyway. Everyone except for me was super excited to play Blob Tag again, so that's what we played, even though I didn't want to. Margot was It, and guess who she tagged first?

Cora.

I watched them hold hands and run around the yard, and I started to feel so sad that I just stopped in my tracks.

My stomach hurt. I sat down next to the fence and waited for Cora to come over and ask me if I was okay. But she didn't even notice. She was too busy laughing her face off like a dumb hyena.

"Miss Conti, are you all right?" came Miss Tibbs's voice.

"Just taking a break," I said as I looked up at her. Miss Tibbs looked different. I looked at her really closely for a few seconds and then I realized what it was.

"Miss Tibbs!" I exclaimed. "You changed your hair!"

Miss Tibbs had always had gray hair cut in exactly the same way—in a bob with a big bunch of bangs. Now her hair was cut in a new way that was much shorter and more stylish. It was also brown!

"It's brown!" I exclaimed.

"The woman at the salon called it 'roasted chestnut,'" Miss Tibbs said. Then she smiled a real, actual smile and fluffed her hair gently, like she was in a shampoo commercial. "Do you like it?"

"I love it!" I gushed. "I really do!"

Three's a Crowd

"Thank you," she said. Then she walked away in the direction of Matthew Sawyer, who was feeding the leftovers of his lunch to a line of ants by the trash can.

What on earth has happened to Miss Tibbs? I wondered. Did someone hypnotize her? Did she swap bodies with someone else, someone very nice and friendly? Why the heck is she so happy?

I wanted to tell Cora all about it. But Cora was still holding hands with Margot at the other end of the playground, far away. Far, far away from me.

Chapter 9

At dismissal, I saw Margot's mom. I knew it was her right away because she had the same orange hair as Margot and she looked super fashionable in high-heeled boots, a purple knitted poncho, and very big, black sunglasses.

She was holding the leash of the most adorable bulldog ever. He had big floppy cheeks that looked really wrinkly and thick brown-and-white fur. His big brown eyes looked so kind and smart. His collar was black leather and had BERNIE written in rhinestones on it.

Three's a Crowd

Even though my feelings were still really hurt and I didn't feel like talking to Margot, I could not resist petting that big bundle of cuteness.

"Is this Bernie?" I asked Margot.

"Yep," she said, smiling. "Watch out. He loves to lick."

I knelt down and scratched Bernie behind the ears. He wagged his tail and licked my arm like it was a big juicy lollipop.

The Fix-It Friends

Right then, Dad walked over to pick up Jude, Ezra, and me. As we walked out of the playground, Dad said he had to stop at the Monroe for a few minutes before we went home.

The Monroe is the building where my dad works as a super. If something breaks, he has to go over and check it out, even if he's not supposed to be working right then.

"Is it a Mr. Luntzgarten problem again?" I asked Dad.

Mr. Luntzgarten is a man who lives on the fourth floor of the Monroe. He's a *curmudgeon*. I love that word because it means exactly what it sounds like—a cranky, crusty grump. Mr. Luntzgarten has no wife and no kids and no pets, and he is retired from his job. That means he has a lot of time to scold people, and the person he likes to scold most is me.

Three's a Crowd

His favorite thing to do, besides scolding me, is calling my dad to tell him about stuff that's broken. Half the time it's not really broken, but my dad always has to check it out anyway because he is a super and that's what supers have to do.

"There's a leak on the seventh floor," said Dad. "For once, it has nothing to do with Mr. Luntzgarten. Actually, I haven't heard from Mr. Luntzgarten in a few weeks—not even to complain about the birds. He always complains about birds chirping outside his window this time of year."

Ezra laughed. Ezra lives in the Monroe, so he knows all about Mr. Luntzgarten and his complaints.

"Hey, can we hang out at my apartment while you check out the leak? I have the key," said Ezra. Except Ezra talks at the speed of light, so it sounded like "Heycanwehangoutatmyapartment (breath) whileyoucheckouttheleak?Ihavethe (breath) key." If you had just met Ezra, you would never understand what he was saying. But I have known him ever since I was a tiny child, so I can understand him with no problem.

"Yes, Ezra's house, pleeeeease?" I asked Dad.

I love hanging out at Ezra's house because:

1. He has the best snacks.

2. He has the cutest cat.

3. He has a computer there, so he can record my demo album.

4. He lets me play with anything I want and never shouts "Get your grubby hands off!" like Jude does. Ezra is way nicer than Jude. Sometimes I wonder how they are friends.

Three's a Crowd

"Sure, if it's okay with your mom," said Dad. Then he said, "Hey, wait a sec. Where's Cora? Isn't she coming, too?"

I shook my head hard. Then I said to Ezra and Jude, "I need to call an emergency meeting of the Fix-It Friends."

"Without Cora?" Ezra asked.

"Definitely without Cora," I said.

On the way over to the Monroe, Dad told me that he'd called the House of Bounce about my birthday party. Great news! We could have the party there in two weeks!

"But we'll have to keep it small," said Dad. "Just a few friends."

"So, like, fifteen people?" I asked him.

"More like five," he replied.

"How about ten?"

"How about eight?" Dad asked. "To match your age?"

I counted the people I'd already invited on my hands. "Cora, Camille, Noah. Minnie—if she's back—Ezra, Jude, Pearl, and me. That's eight. With Margot, it will be nine. I invited her, but I could just uninvite her. After all, we just don't have the room. Nothing personal. I'll tell her tomorrow."

"Well, hold on a sec," said Dad. "We can't uninvite people. And I think it's nice that you invited her. I guess we can make it nine."

"Are you sure?" I asked. "I don't want to break your bank."

"You don't? Then how come you keep asking for a pony and a trip to Disneyland?" Dad chortled with laughter as we walked into the Monroe lobby.

We were getting into the elevator when who should walk in but Mr. Luntzgarten? He looked pretty much the same as always. He was wearing the same black coat with the same brown, checkered hat that makes him look like a person in an old-fashioned black-and-white movie. But his humongous white eyebrows were not all scrunched up the way they usually were. Also, a strange sound was coming from his mouth. Humming!

Mr. Luntzgarten sighs. He groans. He grumbles. He mutters. But he never, ever hums.

Ezra, Jude, Dad, and I were really quiet until Mr. Luntzgarten got off on the fourth floor. Then we burst out talking.

"Am I hearing things? Or was Mr. Luntzgarten just humming a merry tune?" asked Jude.

"Why the heck is Mr. Luntzgarten so cheery?" I asked. "Do you think he won the lottery? Ooooooh, I hope so! Then he might give me a really amazing present for my birthday! Maybe a computer, or a diamond tiara?"

"Nah," said Dad. "There's only one thing that makes a person so happy that they hum a merry tune without even noticing."

"You're right," I said. "I can't believe it! Mr. Luntzgarten GOT A PUPPY!"

Dad shook his head. "He's in love, I bet you anything."

Chapter 10

Dad went to check out the leak downstairs, and we ate snacks in Ezra's kitchen. I drank three glasses of the delicious hibiscus iced tea Ezra's mom always keeps in the fridge while I played with Pep, Ezra's kitten. Pep acted like he thought my hair was yellow yarn and kept swatting at it, which cracked us all up.

When Pep got bored with my hair, I announced, "Okay, guys, let's get down to business! I need to put out a Code Turquoise. I repeat. Code Turquoise. This is not a test. Code Turquoise."

"Remind me," said Ezra. "What's a Code Turquoise?"

"It means that a member of our group is in great danger!" I explained.

"Is this because Cora's been playing with that new girl? Margaret?" Jude asked. "I saw you moping at recess today."

"First of all, her name is Margot! With a silent *T*," I said. "Second of all, yes. Cora has fallen under the spell of that evil sorceress. She spends all her time with Margot! She plays Blob Tag! She's taking swimming lessons! She's even eating SCHOOL LUNCH!"

"You want to issue a state of emergency because Cora is eating school lunch?" Jude joked. "I know school lunch is bad, but it's not *that* bad."

"This is serious!" I exclaimed. "What are we going to do? What's the plan?"

Three's a Crowd

"Look, Ronny—" started Jude.

I cleared my throat, which is the international signal for *How many times have I told you to stop calling me by that dumb, babyish nickname?*

"Okay, fine—*Veronica*," said Jude. "If you're feeling left out, just tell Cora."

"Just tell her that Margot is spinning a web of dark magic to catch her? *Warn* her, you mean?"

"Well, maybe don't use the words 'web of dark magic,'" said Ezra.

"Just tell her that you miss her," said Jude.

"Yeah, keep it simple," said Ezra.

"Have you met my sister?" Jude asked Ezra. "Veronica can't keep anything simple."

I glared at Jude and said to Ezra, "Sure, simple. Got it."

That afternoon, I practiced what I would say to Cora. It was very simple and very polite, and I knew it would work. So after dinner, I called her.

"Hey, V," Mrs. Klein said when she picked up the phone. She never calls me by my name because she says it takes too long. "Why do you think I named the boys Bo and Lou? Shortest names I could think of!" she always says.

"What's cookin'?" she asked.

"Not much," I said. "Is Cora there?"

"Sorry, babe, Cora's not here. Still at that girl's house. What's her name? Marjorie? Marlene?"

Three's a Crowd

"Margot," I said. "But it's almost eight o'clock!"

"Yeah, she stayed for dinner," said Mrs. Klein. "Get a load of this: They were having oysters. Oysters! Hold on a sec."

Suddenly her voice boomed out, "BO, UNTIE YOUR BROTHER THIS INSTANT!" After a few seconds, she boomed, "YOU DID WHAT?" Then after a few more seconds, she shouted, "WITH CRAZY GLUE? AGAIN?"

Then she said to me, "I better go. Want Cora to call you when she gets back?"

"Yes, please."

"You got it, babe," said Mrs. Klein. Then she added, "Hey, V, you sound a little down."

That's the thing about Mrs. Klein. Even though she packs a Loco Lunch Box and never buttons her shirt right, she pays attention to the things that count.

"Everything okay?" she asked.

"No!" I wanted to shout. "Everything is not okay! Your daughter has left me for a new girl who speaks French and eats oysters and puts a zillion zippers on clothes that DON'T EVEN NEED ZIP-PERS! Please do something! I BEG YOU!"

But instead I said, "Oh, I'm fine, thanks."

Before she hung up, I heard her yell at the boys, "WHY IS THE MILK BLUE? KIIIIDS!"

I waited until nine thirty that night for Cora to call me back, but she never did. I wanted to wait even longer, but Mom and Dad forced me to go to sleep.

I woke up in the middle of the night because I had a terrible nightmare. In the dream, I opened my closet and saw my favorite red dress, which my aunt Alice made for me. Only it looked different because there was a big, humongous black zipper in the back. When I unzipped it, guess who was hiding in the dress? Margot!

She jumped out at me. Her orange hair was very long and swirling like octopus tentacles. It reached out and grabbed me. I screamed, but then my mouth turned into a zipper, and Margot zipped it closed. She tied me up with a big, strong strand of her hair and locked me in the closet.

When I woke up, I was so terrified that I crawled into bed with Mom and Dad. I slept in between them for the rest of the night.

Chapter 11

The next morning, I wanted to get to school early to talk to Cora before Margot got there, but I couldn't find my left shoe anywhere! After about a hundred minutes, I found it in Pearl's room in a gift bag left over from Christmas.

"What are you doing with my shoe?" I asked her.

"Is my bifday pwesent!" she said.

Usually, I think Pearl is the cutest thing since the invention of puppy-shaped paper clips. But on this day, I did not think she was cute at all.

I grabbed my shoe out of the bag, and Pearl whined, "Hey! That's my pwesent!"

Three's a Crowd

"It's not your present! It's my shoe!" I snapped, "And, besides, it's not even your birthday!"

Pearl gasped. She learned how to do that from copying me. It's my favorite sound effect.

I shoved my shoe on and walked as fast as I could with Mom and Jude, but we were still late for school. Margot and Cora were already sitting next to each other in Antarctica. They were chatting away, like two little birds tweeting together on a branch. I tried to talk to Wren to show them that I didn't care.

"Good morning, Wren!" I said. "How are you?"

"No comment," he said.

"I wonder how Minnie's doing in Puerto Rico. I hope her *abuela*'s okay. Don't you wish you were in Puerto Rico right now instead of boring old school? Do you think Minnie will ever come back? Do you think she forgot about us?"

"No," he said.

"No to which question?" I asked him.

"No comment," he said.

Margot stayed right next to Cora for the whole morning. She only left our table for a minute to go to the bathroom.

As soon as she got up, Cora said to me, "Veronica, you have to come to Margot's mom's studio! It's *fantastique*! She taught me how to use a sewing machine!"

"Cool," I said, trying to find a way to start the speech I had practiced. But she just kept talking.

"And then we went back to her apartment and—listen to this: She has her own room—"

"That's nice, but—" I tried again.

"—*and* her own bathroom! Can you believe it? I wish I had my own room! It was so nice to have peace and quiet for a change; no little brothers or sisters running around bothering us."

I felt like Cora wasn't just talking about her house but my house, too. After all, I had a little sister that always bothered us. I always thought Cora loved Pearl, but maybe she was tired of her shenanigans.

"And you will never believe what her mom made for dinner," Cora went on.

"Oysters," I said.

"Yes! Oysters, just for a regular Monday dinner! Can you believe it? The fanciest thing my mom makes is PB&J with extra-crunchy peanut butter."

Then Margot came back from the bathroom. I hadn't even had one minute to give Cora my speech! So I decided to talk to her at lunch while Margot waited in line. But that didn't work, either, because Cora said she was getting school lunch again, too, and she went off to wait in line with Margot.

Dad had made one of my favorite sandwiches— a cream-cheese-and-cucumber sandwich with no crust, exactly like what you get when you have royal tea in England—but I only took a few nibbles. I just didn't have my usual appetite.

Margot and Cora were talking all about Margot's mom's new line of kids' clothing. They were chatting so much that it was like they didn't even notice me sitting there. I felt invisible.

"My favorite dress is the black, shiny dress with zippers that go up both sides," Margot said. "Remember that one, Coco?"

I waited for Cora to correct her. But, instead, she smiled and said, "Oh yes, Gogo, that one was my favorite, too."

Three's a Crowd

Coco? I thought. *Gogo?*

My heart was racing, and my face felt very hot. They had nicknames for each other? Nicknames! This was serious. This had gone too far.

I suddenly felt very desperate for Cora to pay attention to me.

"Hey, Cora!" I exclaimed. "We have a Fix-It Friends emergency! It's . . ." I had to think of a good problem, fast. "Maya! It's Maya. She looks worried again. I mean, it's almost spring, which means bugs are buzzing around again, and you know how scared she is of bugs." I was talking really fast, almost as fast as Ezra talks. "I think the Fix-It Friends should have a meeting to help Maya. Immediately."

Cora looked over at the lunch table next to us, where Maya was laughing with the girl next to her.

"She seems fine," said Cora.

"Well, sure, right now," I said. "But worry can strike at any moment."

"What are the Fix-It Friends?" asked Margot.

Finally! Margot was paying attention to *me* for a change.

"It's a problem-solving group," I replied. "I started it. I don't mean to brag, but we're pretty famous."

"So what do you guys do? Solve math problems?" asked Margot.

Three's a Crowd

I laughed really loudly to show how ridiculous that was.

"Not math problems! *Real* problems. Like—Maya. She was so worried about bugs that she couldn't play at recess. It was absolutely awful . . . till we helped her!"

Margot chewed a mouthful of rice and beans.

"Sounds cool," she said. "Can I help?"

"No!" It slipped out before I could stop myself.

"Veronica!" Cora scolded.

I tried to fix things.

"Well, I only mean . . . because, you're so busy, Margot, with swimming and getting used to a new place and everything. The Fix-It Friends is really a big-time commitment."

"I'm not that busy," Margot said. "And it sounds fun."

"Oh, it's not that fun," I said very quickly. "In fact, it's really pretty boring most of the time. A real snooze-fest. My brother is in it, and he's awful! He is so bossy and a know-it-all. Trust me, you'd *hate* it."

"Oh, he's not so bad. And our meetings are a lot of fun," said Cora. Then she started telling Margot all about Maya and Noah and Liv and all the other people we had helped. I took a bite of my sandwich, but I felt like my mouth couldn't chew. It felt like my whole body was made of cement—so heavy and sad.

I'd been trying to find a time to talk to Cora all day, but now I felt like it would be a big waste of time. She'd never listen to me. All she cared about was Margot.

"Lots of people help us all the time," said Cora cheerily. "We love help!"

Three's a Crowd

I couldn't stand the idea of Margot joining the Fix-It Friends. She'd probably just take over and make everyone like her better than me. Even Jude would probably start wearing zippers and speaking French and swimming! Before long, he'd probably want her as his sister instead of me!

No way, I thought. *I'd rather cancel the whole group than let that happen.*

"Actually, Cora, I think you're right about Maya," I said loudly. "She doesn't look worried at all. I was wrong. She doesn't need the Fix-It Friends."

But you do, Cora Klein, I thought. *You do.*

Chapter 12

That day, Nana came with Pearl to pick up Jude, Ezra, and me from school.

"We need an emergency Fix-It meeting," I told them. And then, before they could ask, I said, "No Cora. I'll explain everything at home."

"Wook, Wonny!" shouted Pearl from her stroller. "Is my bifday!"

I looked down and saw that Pearl and Ricardo were both wearing party hats.

"Pearl, you're almost three years old, which is old enough to face the facts," I said firmly. "Your birthday isn't until next month, in April."

Three's a Crowd

Pearl crumpled up in her stroller and started crying.

"I wanna bifday!" she cried. "I wanna 'appy bifday!"

Nana gave me a look that said, *Come on, she's just a poor, defenseless baby!* and I gave her a look that said, *But she's stealing my birthday!*

Pearl just kept crying and drooling all over Ricardo.

So I said very impatiently, "Okay, fine. Happy birthday, Pearl. Happy birthday to you."

She stopped crying and beamed a big smile at me.

"Tank you!" she said oh-so-happily.

When we got home, I went into the kitchen to make some snacks. Pearl walked in with a roll of toilet paper that she pretended was a birthday cake. She sat down in the corner with Ricardo and had a pretend party.

"Yuuuuuum," she said, smacking her lips as she pretended to take a big bite out of the cake. "Faiwy-dust spwinkles!"

No wonder Cora doesn't want to come over here anymore, I thought.

I carried my special nacho snacks into the bedroom I share with Jude. He and Ezra were sitting on the floor, reading comic books.

Jude peered at the plate through his glasses. "What kind of nachos are these?"

Three's a Crowd

"I'm glad you asked," I said. "This is artichoke hearts mashed up into little bits with a fork. You can scoop it up with the nachos. I call it the Broken Hearts Special."

Jude groaned. "Let me guess. This snack has a whole long story to go with it."

"Correct!" I said. I put the plate on the floor and sat cross-legged next to it. As we munched, I gave them an update about Cora's problem.

"It won't work to talk to her! Something more drastic must be done!"

I tapped the floor with my fingertips. Tapping helps me think. Jude says it's very annoying, but I think that his way of thinking, which is to be totally silent, is very annoying. In fact, there is nothing that bothers me more than the sound of no sounds.

"Think!" I told them. "We have to help Cora!"

Jude looked at Ezra. Ezra looked at Jude. I hate it when they do this. It means they are about to say something that I do not want to hear.

"Cora's not the one with the problem," said Jude. "You are."

I snorted.

"That's a laugh!" I said. "Cora's changing faster than a mealworm turning into a beetle, and *I'm* the one with a problem! *Me?* Ha! Ha HA! HA HA HA!"

"Tell her about Arnie-geddon," Jude said to Ezra.

"Yes," agreed Ezra. "It's time."

"What are you talking about?" I asked.

"You must have patience. All will be revealed," said Jude, popping a nacho into his mouth.

"Okay, let me break it down for you," said Ezra, cracking his knuckles. I sat up and paid attention, because when Ezra cracks his knuckles, it means he's going to tell a story, and when Ezra tells a story, you better listen up, or you won't understand a thing. "So, basically, Jude and I had been best friends since the beginning of first grade, and everything was cool until we started second grade and Jude met Arnie."

"Arnie was really funny," added Jude. "He used to do this hilarious routine where he made one of his hands talk to the other hand in funny accents. The best one was his leprechaun voice."

"His leprechaun voice was all wrong," grumbled Ezra. "It didn't sound Irish! It sounded like it was from Transylvania."

"Agree to disagree," said Jude, laughing.

"So anyway . . . Jude suddenly wanted to do everything with Arnie. Lunch with Arnie and recess with Arnie and—oh!" Ezra turned to Jude. "Remember how you were too scared to sleep over at my house, but you went over to Arnie's house and had your first sleepover there?"

I gasped. "Jude, you traitor!"

Ezra continued. "I was so furious at Arnie that once I shoved him really hard at recess and he scraped his elbow, and I got sent to the principal's office, which was really awkward—"

"Because she's your mom!" I laughed.

"Yeah, because of that," Ezra said. "So I fought with Jude, and I fought with Arnie, and it was all a big mess. It was Arnie-geddon . . . until Miss Tibbs saved the day by getting me to play tag at recess with a bunch of other kids. At first I really didn't want to, but it was actually really fun. And in a few days I stopped caring so much about Jude playing with Arnie."

Three's a Crowd

"Yeah, and by that time I was starting to get annoyed by Arnie anyway. He couldn't keep a secret. He told the whole second grade that I was terrified of butterflies. Which I *specifically* told him never to tell anyone!"

"So *that's* why everyone used to tease you about caterpillars," I said.

Jude nodded and then said, "So now do you understand? What is the moral of our tale?"

"Never tell anyone you're scared of butterflies," I said.

"Ummm . . . not exactly," said Ezra.

"Okay then. The moral is: Never be scared of butterflies in the first place because, come on, that's just silly."

Jude sighed. "The point is that you can't force Cora not to play with Margot. You can't control other people."

"Well, that's just not true at all," I said. "Haven't you ever heard of hypnosis?"

"You're going to hypnotize Cora?" Jude raised his eyebrows.

"It's an idea," I said. "I'm full of ideas. They don't call me the president of the Fix-It Friends for nothing."

"Nobody calls you that," Jude said. "Not one single person."

Three's a Crowd

"Just give Cora some space," said Ezra. "Leave her alone for a few days."

"Orrrrrrrr," I said, getting excited, "I could just try to be more fun! More fun than Margot."

Jude and Ezra shook their heads.

But I ignored them. I mean, they're smart and everything, but that doesn't mean they're always right.

Chapter 13

The next morning, as I ate my cereal, I said to my mom, "Instead of having my birthday at the House of Bounce, can we have it at Disneyland?"

Mom laughed. Then she looked at my face and said, "Oh, you're serious?"

"Fine," I sighed. "How about Las Vegas?"

Mom blinked slowly. "In Nevada?"

"I don't know where it is!" I said, annoyed. "I just know you can win a lot of money there! I think you can maybe ride elephants, too. Can we take Cora?"

My mom put her hand on my forehead. "Are you feeling okay, honey?" she asked.

Three's a Crowd

"Just because I want to ride an elephant and win a lot of money so my birthday can be special, you think I'm sick? It's no wonder my friends don't want to come here! We never do anything fun!" And I stormed into my room to get dressed for school.

Mom came into my room a minute later.

"Do you want to talk about what's bothering you?" she asked.

I did. I really did. My mom is a therapist, and her whole entire job is to listen to people talk about their problems and try to make them feel okay.

But Mom is always telling me how important it is to be kind, and I thought she'd be disappointed in me because Margot was new and homesick and I wasn't being very kind to her. So I just shook my head.

"Anything I can do to help?" she asked.

I thought for a second. "Do you have any clothes with a lot of zippers that I could borrow?"

Mom poked around in the dustiest corner of her closet and found her old motorcycle jacket. It was black leather and covered with cool zippers.

"This used to be my all-time favorite." She smiled. "I haven't worn it since I was . . . oh, probably since I was a teenager."

She slid the jacket onto my shoulders and rolled up the sleeves. "It's a little big on you, but I think it looks kind of great."

"KIND of great?" I asked, looking in the mirror. "It looks awesome. It looks Tough with a capital *T*. A not-silent *T*. Thanks, Mom!"

Three's a Crowd

* * *

I skipped into my classroom. I didn't hang my zip-tastic jacket on the wall hook. I decided to keep it on all day. I couldn't wait for Margot and Cora to see it!

I sat down and turned to Wren, who was sharpening his pencil.

"Like my jacket?" I asked him.

"No comment," he replied.

"I'll take that as a yes!" I said. After all, I was an optimist.

But just then is when I stopped being an optimist. Because just then is when I heard giggling and saw Margot and Cora walking through the door, side by side.

At first, I thought my eyes were playing tricks on me. Instead of a pleated dress or poofy skirt, Cora was wearing jeans. I didn't think she even *owned* jeans! Her jacket was unzipped, and, underneath it, I could see she was wearing a T-shirt. A bright green T-shirt.

Margot was wearing the exact same one.

Well, not the *exact* same one. The four sparkly white letters on the front were different. Margot's letters said GOGO and Cora's said COCO.

I sat in my seat and did not move a muscle. My whole body felt frozen and stiff. I felt like I was in Antarctica for real and had been turned to ice.

Chapter 14

When I unfroze, I marched right over to Cora and hissed, "I need to talk to you!"

So we asked Miss Mabel if we could go to the bathroom. I stormed into the hallway with Cora behind me.

"Are you okay?" she asked. Her big brown eyes were worried. "What's wrong?"

I could not believe she didn't already know. "You and Margot are wearing matching outfits! You changed your name to match hers!"

"Oh, this?" laughed Cora, looking down at her shirt. "Margot's mom made it for me. I had to wear it. I didn't want to be rude. But I didn't think it would hurt your feelings. It's just a T-shirt!"

"Ever since Margot got here, it's been 'Margot this' and 'Margot that'! And you're acting different! You're acting like her!"

"I'm just being nice to her because she's new!" Cora protested. She was tugging on her curls, which is what she does when she gets nervous. "Miss Mabel told me to!"

"Yeah, but Miss Mabel didn't tell you to ditch me!" I exclaimed. "She didn't tell you to be an awful friend!"

My voice started to shake a little at the last part because I felt so sorry for myself.

"That's a terrible thing to say!" said Cora. Her eyes filled up with tears. "You're being so mean!"

"ME?" I saw Miss Mabel's face peek out from the classroom, so I stopped shouting and started

angry-whispering. "If I'm so *mean*, then maybe we just shouldn't be friends anymore!"

I didn't want to say it. I only said it because I wanted Cora to say, "What? No! Never! That would be the worst thing in the whole world! We'll always be best friends!"

Instead she said, "Maybe you're right. Maybe we shouldn't be friends anymore."

Then she turned around and walked back into the classroom.

For a second, I just stood there in the hallway.

Then, all of a sudden, a big wave of sadness hit me. I felt like a sand castle getting smashed by a tsunami. I felt so terribly hurt and lonely, and I knew that in about two seconds, I would start to cry. So I ran as fast as I could to the bathroom. I locked myself in the stall, and I cried and cried for a long time.

I was in there for so long that Miss Mabel came in to check on me.

"Hey, lady," she said, knocking on the stall I was in. "The rest of the class has gone off to music. Are you okay in there?"

I came out of the stall and walked over to the sink to splash some water on my face.

"I think life would be easier without friends," I told Miss Mabel, "because they just hurt your feelings and make you feel bad."

"You know what I think?" asked Miss Mabel. "I think sometimes friendships feel so simple, like the easiest thing in the world, and other times, they feel really, really hard."

"This is one of those hard times," I said, drying my face with a paper towel.

Miss Mabel was quiet for a minute. Then she said, "Hey, would you do me a favor? Mr. Aguta really needs some help with his kindergarten science classes this morning. They're making scented playdough, and you know how much those little ones like to eat playdough."

"They do," I sniffed. "They really do."

I spent all morning with the kindergartners. I looked at those happy five-year-old faces and thought, *Life's just easy-peasy for them. No backstabbing, no heartbreak.*

"Enjoy it while you can, kids," I said under my breath. "Enjoy it while you can."

Chapter 15

By the time I was done helping Mr. Aguta, it was time for recess. I stood by the fence and watched Cora and Margot play hopscotch in their matching T-shirts, with matching smiles on their faces.

I figured Miss Tibbs would come over and tell me to "do something productive," but Miss Tibbs was not paying the slightest bit of attention to me. She was doing something I had never seen her do before. She was talking on her phone—and smiling! Matthew Sawyer dropped a granola bar wrapper right next to her, and she didn't even make him pick it up!

Three's a Crowd

What is the world coming to? I thought.

Ezra and Jude walked up to me.

"Hey, are you okay?" asked Ezra.

"Some people have all the luck!" I complained. "Some people have been to Disneyland a billion times and have orange hair and their own rooms and adorable dogs *and* cool nicknames."

"Play tag with us. Whatever kind you want," said Jude.

"I don't want to play tag!" I exclaimed. "What I want is a new best friend. If Cora has one, then I should, too—"

"Calm down, Ron—Veronica," said Jude.

"Cora thinks she's sooooooo special that I could never replace her. Ha! I can replace her in a second! There are plenty of kids *exactly* like Cora."

At just that moment, who should pass by but Camille, dribbling a basketball.

"Hiya," she said in her low, raspy voice.

"Eureka!" I shrieked.

Camille would be the perfect new BFF. She was exactly like her twin sister—only completely different!

I ran over to Camille and threw my arms around her.

Jude and Ezra just shook their heads and walked off.

"Cama Lama Ding Dong!" I squealed.

Three's a Crowd

Camille looked around her and then she said, "Oh. You're talking to me?"

I laughed loudly. "Of course, silly! Don't you like your nickname?"

"A nickname's usually shorter than the real name," said Camille.

"Okay, Camelia Bedelia!" I said as I slung my arm around her shoulder.

"That's still way longer," she said.

"You're so funny!" I cackled. "So what should we play today?"

"I'm just shooting hoops," she said. "I know it's not really your thing."

"GREAT!" I said very loudly so Margot and Cora could hear me. "I just LOVE shooting hoops!"

I took a few steps back and opened my arms wide. "I'm open! Pass it!"

So she passed me the ball. And I kicked it back to her. I thought I did a pretty good job.

"Um, Veronica?" she said. "You don't kick a basketball."

"Sorry Camill-eon." I laughed loudly. "Get it? Like the lizard?"

I looked over to the spot where Cora and Margot were, but they were not paying any attention to me. Not at all! So I grabbed Camille's hand and dragged her over closer to them.

"Let's play tag instead!" Margot and Cora were still not looking at me, so I shouted, "I KNOW A NEW GAME. IT'S CALLED BFF TAG! FOR BEST FRIENDS ONLY! SO IT'S GREAT FOR ME AND YOU, MY BEST FRIEND, RIGHT . . . CACA?"

Camille shook me off.

"Caca?" she said. "What kind of a nickname is that?"

"Cora is Coco, so I thought—"

"I don't know what's going on with you and Cora, but this is too weird for me. I'm not just a Cora substitute, you know!"

And then, to my amazement, she ran off.

To my greater amazement, Margot and Cora walked over to me then.

"Veronica, I think there's been a misunderstanding," Margot said. "I'm really not trying to steal your BFF."

"Yes, Cora is my BFF," I said, "but only if those letters stand for 'Baddest Friend Forever.' So you can steal her all you want. Because she and I broke up."

Cora gasped. This made me furious! She learned that sound effect from me!

"Good!" Cora said.

"Great!" I said back.

"Okay, I think everyone should just cool down down down," Margot said.

"I have never been so happy to not be friends with someone in my whole life!" growled Cora.

"Me too!" I shouted. "Now I don't have to pretend to like the terrible clothes you make."

She gasped again. "And now I don't have to pretend to like your horrible singing, which sounds like a cat crying!"

Then it was my turn to gasp. My heart was racing a million miles a minute, and I felt kind of dizzy.

"Cora Klein," I growled at her. "I hate you!"

I was so furious that I stamped my foot as hard as I could. But instead of stomping the ground, my foot stomped on something slippery—the granola bar wrapper that Miss Tibbs hadn't made Matthew Sawyer pick up. Before I knew what was

happening, I was falling forward. My hands shot out in front of me, and that's when I felt an awful, terrible pain in my left wrist.

I must have screamed really loudly, because a whole bunch of kids crowded around me, including Jude and Ezra. Then Miss Tibbs pushed through and looked at my wrist.

"It may be broken," she said. "We'll go to the nurse's office, and I'll call your parents."

Chapter 16

"Ronny, honey!" said Mom as she rushed into the nurse's office. I didn't even care that she was calling me by my dumb nickname because I was so relieved to see her.

We took a taxi to the hospital, and that's when I knew it was serious; Mom never lets us take taxis.

Dad was already waiting for us in the emergency room, and they both stayed by my side when the doctor examined me.

Guess what?

I *did* break my wrist. Well, I fractured it.

"Will I ever write again?" I asked the doctor in a whisper. He had wild, wispy white hair that stuck straight up, which reminded me of Albert Einstein. That made me think he was really smart and knew what he was doing.

"Aren't you right-handed?" asked the doctor.

I nodded.

"Well, then, you can write now. The cast is only going on your left wrist." He smiled. "You'll need it on for four weeks or so. Then you'll be as good as new. Plus, you can pick out the color you want your cast to be."

They didn't have turquoise, but they did have baby blue, which was the next best thing.

"You can have all your friends sign their names," said the doctor. He thought this would cheer me up, but it just made me think of Cora.

My wrist was broken.

My friendship was broken.

It felt like everything was broken. Too broken for even me to fix it.

Chapter 17

It didn't take long for me to find the silver lining to my broken wrist. I got to stay home from school! For four days!

The doctor said I could go back to school after a day, but I convinced Mom to let me stay home on Friday for an extra day. I told her my wrist hurt a lot, which was true. But what hurt even worse were my feelings. I did not want to see Cora Klein ever again. Or Margot. And I definitely didn't want to see them hopscotching happily ever after together.

On those days home from school, I stayed at Nana and Nonno's house. It's my favorite thing to do because they spoil me rotten.

Nana made me alphabet soup and chocolate milk shakes every day.

Nonno taught me how to play games with an Italian deck of cards, which is much cooler than a regular deck. Instead of just hearts or spades, there are pictures of vicious snakes and stuff.

Nana even let me drink peppermint tea out of her special china cups from Italy.

"Your-a birthday's-a comin' up-a!" she said as we sipped. "Party-a time!"

"I may not have a party this year, Nana," I said sadly.

"No?" she asked. "Why-a not?"

"Well, I can't jump on the trampoline with this cast on, so I have to cancel the whole party. Plus,

Minnie's in Puerto Rico, and Cora's . . ." I trailed off. "Cora's gone, too."

"Don't-a worry, *bella*," said Nana, hugging me so close that I could smell her nice perfume and feel her pearls pressing into my forehead. "It's-a gonna be O-a K-a."

On Monday, after four fun days at home, Mom woke me up and told me to get dressed for school.

"Oh, but my wrist!" I protested. "I better take one more day off just to be sure I'm really recovered."

Mom said, "Nice try, kiddo." Then she pulled the covers all the way off me. "Hop to it!"

But I didn't hop to it. I lay in my bottom bunk, moaning to myself.

Jude came in and said, "Are you throwing yourself a pity party?"

"Yes," I said. "My birthday party's canceled, so I might as well just have a pity party instead." I moaned some more. "What am I going to do at recess? It's going to be so terrible."

Jude sighed and groaned and then he said, "Fine—Ezra and I will play with you. Happy now?"

"Not really," I said. "Because you act like it's just a huge favor."

Jude sighed and groaned again and said in a funny voice, "Veronica Laverne Conti, won't you please grant us the pleasure of your company today at recess? It would be an honor."

Three's a Crowd

I raised my eyebrows. "Was that your leprechaun voice?"

"Yeah," said Jude. "Arnie taught it to me."

"Ezra's right. It is terrible."

Jude threw a stuffed animal at me and laughed. I laughed, too. It felt better to have a plan for recess. Even if that plan involved my brother.

Chapter 18

When I walked into the classroom that morning, I saw that Miss Mabel had rearranged all the seats at all the tables. I was so relieved. Cora was in South America. Margot was in Europe. I was in Africa.

Wren had moved to Africa with me. I was happy that he was still sitting next to me. When you think of it, Wren is a relaxing person to be around. He is very predictable.

"Hi, Wren," I said. "Anything exciting happen while I was gone?"

"Yes," he replied.

Three's a Crowd

I figured that was all he would say, but he kept talking. "Cora cried a lot the day you went to the hospital and so did Margot, and then the next day Miss Mabel changed all the tables. Also my dad decided not to be an accountant anymore, and instead he is going to be a pastry chef."

I was absolutely dumbfounded. I guess Wren wasn't so predictable after all.

"Want to sign my cast?" I asked him.

"Yes," he said.

Other kids had written little messages or pictures or signed their whole names, but Wren just wrote "Wren."

"Hey, can I sign?" asked Matthew Sawyer, and I said, "Sure." He was sitting in Africa, too. I thought he was going to write something dumb, like "Smell you later," but he just wrote, "Feel better soon. Matthew Whitman Sawyer."

He felt really bad because it had been his granola bar wrapper that made me slip and break my wrist, so he was extra nice. Plus, he knows a lot of helpful tips about caring for broken bones because his mom is a doctor.

"If it gets really itchy, you could stick a chopstick inside to scratch it," he said. "It works really well."

"Hey, that's a really good idea," I said. "Thanks."

In fact, everyone was extra nice to me, even Miss Tibbs. At recess, she zipped up my jacket for me, because zipping jackets is one of those things you really need two hands for, like opening thermoses and putting tops on markers.

As she zipped up my jacket, I looked closely at Miss Tibbs.

She was wearing her usual black coat, but underneath I saw a glimpse of red peeking through.

Miss Tibbs never wore red. Miss Tibbs never wore green. Miss Tibbs never wore any color at all. Only black.

Curiouser and curiouser, I thought.

Then I noticed what Miss Tibbs was wearing on her head.

A hat. A brown, checkered hat. The old-fashioned kind that looks like it belongs in a black-and-white movie.

I have only seen one other person wearing that kind of hat.

Seymour Luntzgarten!

That's when I remembered how I had introduced the two of them at the memorial for Ezra's guinea pig. They had also both signed the petition I made to get Miss Mabel a new speaker. And I definitely remember Miss Tibbs writing down Mr. Luntzgarten's phone number on a piece of paper and slipping it in her pocket.

Those sneaky suckers! They'd fallen in love!

"I like your hat, Miss Tibbs," I said. "Is it new?"

"Yes, or, rather, no," she stammered. "Yes and no, I suppose. It's an old hat but new to me. A friend gave it to me."

Bingo!

I could just hear the wedding bells ringing! And if Miss Tibbs and Mr. Luntzgarten got married, I'd definitely be the flower girl! At the party, grumpy old Mr. Luntzgarten would give a toast and say, "The true hero tonight is Veronica Laverne Conti. Without her, none of this would be possible. Three cheers for Veronica!" There would not be a dry eye in the place.

"What's your favorite kind of flower, Miss Tibbs?" I asked.

"I'm not sure," she replied. "Daisies, perhaps. Or mums. Why?"

"Oh, no reason." I smiled. "You know, I'm right-handed. That means my broken wrist does not stop me from doing things like writing or brushing my teeth or, I don't know . . . sprinkling flower petals."

Miss Tibbs looked really confused, but she just said, "I'm glad, Miss Conti."

That's when Jude came over to play with me, just like he'd promised he would. But it wasn't just him. All the Fix-It Friends came, too, including our clients. Cora wasn't there of course, but I hardly even noticed because I was so happy to see Liv and Maya and Noah and even J.J. Taylor.

"Hi, guys! What are you all doing here?" I asked.

"Jude and Ezra said you could use some company," said J.J.

"We're here," said Liv, doing a pirouette, "for cheer!"

She did a ballet kick and landed in a *ta-da!* position.

"What do you want to play?" asked Maya in her small, whispery voice.

"Well, that's the problem," I said. "I can't play much with this broken wrist."

"Umm, *problem*? Did someone say *problem*?" asked Jude, raising his eyebrows. "Because I happen to be the president of a world-famous problem-solving group—"

Three's a Crowd

I giggled. "Jude! Cut it out!"

The Fix-It Friends don't have a president. And if we did, of course, it would be me!

"So you can't do much with your broken wrist," said Ezra, "but you *can* talk, can't you?"

"Trust me," said Jude, rolling his eyes. "She can talk, all right."

"So how about a few rounds of a little game I like to call . . ." Ezra paused to make sure I was full of anticipation. ". . . 'Would You Rather?'"

"Yes!" I squealed. "You're a genius!"

It was the perfect idea. I have always loved playing "Would You Rather?" but I could never play with Cora because she just doesn't get it.

I'd ask her, "Would you rather have the ability to fly or breathe underwater?"

"Oooooh, I can't choose!" she'd say. "They're both so wonderful!"

And when she would pick the choices, it was worse, because she always made it too easy by making one choice terrible and the other one great, like, "Would you rather eat boiled worms or a hot-fudge sundae with extra whipped cream?"

But Jude and Ezra are experts at "Would You Rather?" So we all sat down on the ground and played.

Three's a Crowd

"Would you rather eat your favorite food for breakfast, lunch, and dinner for the rest of your life," asked Ezra, "or never eat it ever again?"

"Never eat it again," said Jude. "Then I'd always have great memories and never get sick of it."

"Are you kidding?" I said. "Eat it for every meal! You can't get enough of a good thing!"

Liv piped up then. "Would you rather get stung by a swarm of bees or pinched by a bunch of hermit crabs?"

"Crabs!" Maya said quickly. She is terrified of bugs.

"No way!" came Matthew Sawyer's voice. A second later, he plopped down next to Maya. "I'd rather get bee stings, for sure. Some people think bee venom can be used as medicine, you know. For arthritis and stuff. My mom told me about it."

"Can bees cure a broken wrist?" I asked.

"I don't think so," said Matt.

"Then I agree with Maya," I said. "Crabs! A pinch isn't so bad. After all, my grandparents pinch my cheeks all the time!"

We had so much fun that I sat next to Matt during lunch and kept playing. Wren sat with us, too. He didn't ask any questions, but he was good at making choices lightning fast, without any explanations. He'd just spit out the answers, very sure of himself.

"Porcupine poop."

"Bed of nails."

"Zombie puppet."

I saw that Margot and Cora were eating school lunch together at the other end of the table, but, after a while, I didn't even notice them.

Chapter 19

The next morning, a miracle happened! When I walked into the classroom, there was Minnie! She had finally come back from Puerto Rico!

"Minerva Ramos!" I shrieked. "Am I ever glad to see you!"

She said her *abuela* was feeling a lot better, which is why they had come home.

Then she had a million questions for me, like why was I wearing a blue cast? And who was the new girl? And why weren't Cora and I saying one word to each other?

"It's a long story," I said. "A tale of heartbreak, betrayal, and one slippery granola bar wrapper. Oh, and, by the way, Miss Tibbs is in love. And Wren's dad is now a pastry chef."

"What was he before?" she asked.

"An accountant."

"Huh," said Minnie. "I go away for two weeks and everything gets turned upside down."

That night after dinner, Mom said, "I know we had to cancel the trampoline party, but I think we should still have your birthday party on Saturday. We'll just do it here!"

"We'll see," I said.

This time, "We'll see" did not mean "You betcha." It meant "why bother?"

Mom wanted to tell me her ideas to make the party fun, but I didn't feel like talking about it. The next night was the same thing, and the night after that was, too. I knew Cora wouldn't be there, and I just couldn't imagine a birthday party without Cora.

On Friday, I went to Minnie's house after school. We wrote a new song for my demo album, *One Tough Cookie.* Minnie wrote the music part on her piano, and I wrote the words. It was a slow, sad song called "Three's a Crowd."

When Dad and I got home, Jude and Ezra rushed to the door to meet me.

"Close your eyes!" Ezra told me. Then Jude took my right hand and led me into the house.

"Now, open!" said Jude.

I blinked a few times. I was in our living room, only it didn't really look like our living room. It looked like the bottom of a swimming pool. There were tons of turquoise streamers everywhere—crisscrossing the ceiling and hanging down in

strands from the lamps and television and paint-
ings. Everywhere I turned, there were turquoise balloons floating against the ceiling, with turquoise
ribbons hanging off of them like tails. There was
even a whole line of turquoise party hats waiting
on the mantle.

On the wall above the sofa hung a homemade
sign decorated with turquoise glitter. I recognized
Jude's handwriting right away. It said:

Three's a Crowd

Happy 8th birthday, Ronny Bo Bonny!!

And there, standing next to the sign, were Jude and Ezra and Pearl, who had a big smudge of turquoise glitter on her cheek and a balloon in each hand.

"Wowza," I said.

"Wowza," repeated Pearl.

"It's for your party tomorrow," Jude said. "Do you like it? Ezra and I might have gotten a little

carried away with the streamers, but I figured that's just how you like it."

"We've got the entertainment all covered, too," said Ezra in a rush. "I'm gonna deejay, and we'll do freeze dancing and a limbo contest and then, of course, the piñata."

"Oh, Mom never lets us have piñatas," I said. "She says they're a one-way ticket to the emergency room."

"See for yourself," said Jude, pointing into the hallway.

There was Mom, on a stepladder, hanging a big, white poodle piñata from a hook in the ceiling.

"I thought we'd try it just this once," said Mom, smiling.

I looked around at Mom and Ezra and Jude and Dad and Pearl. They were all looking at me with big hopeful smiles on their faces. I knew how much they all wanted to make me happy. And I liked the streamers and balloons and party hats and especially the piñata—I really did. But the truth was that I just didn't feel cheerful.

"Thanks," I said. I wanted to say it with a lot of pep, but it came out kind of weak. I tried to say it again, with more excitement, but when I opened my mouth, a loud sobbing sound slipped out. Before I knew it, fat, hot tears were sliding down my face.

I ran upstairs as fast as I could, into my bedroom. I threw myself facedown on my bed and cried louder than I had ever cried before.

A minute later, I heard footsteps. I knew they were Mom's because they were slow and soft. Then I felt a hand on my back and Mom's voice saying, "Oh, honey."

"I like the decorations," I sobbed, "but it's not really a party without Cora."

Except I was crying so hard, it just came out: "I like the WAAAAAAAA, but it's not WAAAAAA without WAAAAAAAAAAAAAAA!"

"Honey, I'm having trouble understanding you," said Mom. "Is this about Cora? Did you two have a fight?"

I was crying too hard to answer, so I just nodded really fast.

"Because of the new girl?"

I nodded again.

"Did the green-eyed monster rear its head?"

This made me so surprised that I looked up.

"How'd you know Margot has green eyes? You've never even met her."

Mom laughed. "Margot's not the green-eyed monster," Mom said. "I'm talking about jealousy. That's what Shakespeare called it."

"I guess I'm jealous," I sniffled, sitting up on the bed. "But how would you feel if some new girl showed up speaking French and wearing zippers and eating *oysters* and stole your best friend?"

"I'd feel really jealous," said Mom, squeezing my hand, "and probably a little heartbroken."

"I just don't understand what I did to make Cora not like me anymore," I said.

I laid my head on Mom's lap, and she twirled my hair like I used to do to myself when I was a baby, sucking on my paci. It still makes me feel oh-so-calm and peaceful.

"You didn't do anything wrong," Mom said.

"Well, I kind of did," I replied. "I told Cora the clothes she makes are ugly and also that I hate her."

Mom and I both laughed at the same time.

"Okay, so maybe you did a few things wrong," she said. "But so what? You're human. What I mean is that it's not your fault that Cora made a new friend. It's not because of anything you did. And it doesn't mean she doesn't like you anymore."

"I just want things to go back to the way they used to be." I grabbed a tissue and blew my nose hard.

"The thing about friendships is that they can't stay the same forever. How could they? People change, and friendships have to change, too. But that's not always a bad thing."

"It feels bad," I said. "It feels awful. I don't even think I'm an optimist anymore. Because I don't think this will have a happy ending."

"I don't know about that," said Mom. "Sometimes friends grow apart and move on. Sometimes, you just need some space before you find your way back together . . . and I have a feeling it's going to be that way with Cora."

"You do?" I asked hopefully.

"I really do," she replied. "It's just my mom-stinct."

"You know, Mom," I said. "You're pretty good at problem-solving. You're almost Fix-It Friend material. *Almost.*"

Chapter 20

The next morning, I woke up to the most delicious smell in the world. Fresh, hot waffles! With strawberries! And whipped cream!

Dad always makes me breakfast in bed on my birthday. Then he serves it on a real tray. I love it! It makes me feel like a queen.

Pearl was still sleeping, and we just let her sleep. But the smell woke Jude up, and he climbed down from the top bunk to sit on the foot of my bed, where he stole whipped cream–covered strawberries from my plate.

Mom and Dad sat next to my bed, and while I

ate, they told me the story of the day I was born. They tell it to me every year. It's an exciting story because it starts with a huge snowstorm.

Nobody thought there would be a big snowstorm because it was the end of March, but—surprise! Blizzard!

Then came the next surprise: Even though I wasn't supposed to be born for two more weeks, my mom started having contractions, which is

how you know that a baby's going to be born. It was late at night, and my mom woke up my dad.

"The baby's coming!" she said.

"I know, in two weeks," he said. He was still half asleep.

"No! She's coming right now!" my mom said.

"She can't come right now. We're in the middle of a blizzard!" my dad said.

This is Jude's favorite part of the story. He always says, "See? Even then you had no patience! And you were already a drama queen."

So, Mom and Dad had Nana and Nonno come downstairs to babysit Jude, who was only two years old. Then Dad tried to dig the car out from under all the snow so they could drive to the hospital. But it was freezing, and the snow had turned icy, and it was taking too long.

Three's a Crowd

"It's taking too long!" my mom shouted. "We have to go to the hospital now!"

They had no idea how they would get there. It was way too far to walk, especially in the snow. The subways weren't working because of the blizzard. And there were no taxis anywhere.

"Did you panic?" I always ask Mom.

"A little," she said, "but I knew everything would be all right."

"How? How'd you know?"

"Mom-stinct," she always says.

So Dad kept shoveling the snow off the car while Mom waited in the entryway to our building. The contractions kept coming, and she knew she didn't have much time before the baby, who was me, would be born. And then, suddenly, a birthday miracle happened.

A limousine passed right by our building. It was white and really, really long. Dad ran up to it and waved his arms. This is my favorite part of the story.

The limo stopped, and inside were a bride and groom who had just gotten married! They were driving home from their wedding party.

"My wife's having a baby! Right now!" Dad said. "Can you give us a lift?"

The bride and groom said, "Sure. Why not?"

Just an hour after that I was born, safe and sound, in the hospital.

Mom and Dad were so grateful to that nice couple that they named me after them. Dad always jokes that they were going to name me after the groom. If they had, right now I'd be Herbert Ewell Conti. That's Dad's favorite part of the story.

Three's a Crowd

But they didn't name me after the groom. They named me after the bride. Her name was Veronica.

And when Mom said my name to just-born me, they knew it was the right name because I grinned a big grin. And even though everyone else thought it was just gas, Mom knew. She just knew. That's her favorite part of the story. She always gets a tear in her eye when she tells it.

"I can't believe that was eight years ago today," said Mom, giving me a squeeze. "Happy birthday, honey."

Pearl ran in then. She ran so fast that her PJ pants dropped down to her ankles. She yanked them up and then she yanked out her paci and shouted, "'APPY BIFDAY TO ME!"

"Pearl, my girl," said Dad. "It's not your birthday—"

"It's okay, Dad," I said. "I just thought of something."

Then I turned to Pearl and made my eyes very wide. "Hey, Pearly Pie, you know what I just realized?"

She made her eyes very wide, too, and said, "What?"

"Today's your un-birthday!"

"It *is*?" she said.

"It is!" I cried. "It really is!"

She clapped in glee.

"Now close your eyes, and I'll give you a bite of your un-birthday cake."

She squeezed her little blue eyes closed and opened her mouth wide. I popped in a bite of waffle, all soggy with syrup.

"Yummmmm," she said as she chewed. "Butterfwy-miwk icing!"

Three's a Crowd

Then I popped a strawberry slice with whipped cream into her mouth.

"Faiwy-dust spwinkles!" she said with her mouth full.

Just then, the doorbell rang.

"Now who on earth could that be?" Mom asked. She is a terrible faker, and I knew that she knew who it was. I ran to answer the door.

There, on my doorstep, were Cora and her mom.

Chapter 21

Cora's mom was holding an enormous shopping bag with a huge red bow taped onto it.

"Happy birthday, V!!" said Mrs. Klein.

I opened the door wider to let them in.

"Hi," Cora squeaked, giving me a little wave.

"Hi," I said back.

"I know your party isn't till later, but Cora wants to talk," said Mrs. Klein.

Mrs. Klein huffed and puffed up the stairs to my room, holding the enormous shopping bag. She placed it carefully in the corner next to Jude's desk, where he was reading *Mummy Knows Best: Tales from the Crypt*.

"I'm going to see if your mom has any coffee," she said. "Jude, babe, come downstairs and tell me all about that book. What is that—science fiction?"

Jude jumped up. He was excited that someone actually wanted to hear about his book.

"See, that's a common mistake," he said. "This genre is actually more *horror* fiction. Let me explain. . . ."

I rolled my eyes.

Cora laughed. Then we both sat cross-legged on the floor and were quiet for a long time.

Finally, Cora asked, "How's your wrist?"

"It doesn't really hurt anymore," I said. "But it gets really itchy, so I scratch it with a chopstick."

We got quiet again. I didn't know what to say to Cora because I didn't know if she was still my friend or not.

"I know you're really mad at me—" she started to say.

I interrupted her. "I'm not mad. I was, but I'm not anymore."

Cora nodded. "Me too."

"I was just mad because I thought you didn't like me anymore."

"But that's not true at all!" Cora protested. "I did like you. I still do! I didn't want to replace you with Margot. I just wanted to make a new friend."

"But Margot is so fascinating and exciting, and I just felt so . . . so . . . boring."

"You're the opposite of boring!" Cora laughed. "You were basically born in a limousine!"

"I didn't mean what I said about the clothes you make," I said, feeling embarrassed. "I like them."

Cora nodded. "I'm really sorry I insulted your singing. I think you're going to be a star one day. Really!"

"Cora," I said. "I know we broke up, but do you want to un-break up? I mean, do you want to be friends again?"

"Yes," she said. "I really, really, really do."

"Me too!" I exclaimed. "I really, really, really, *really* do!"

We both burst out laughing.

"But what about Margot?" I asked.

"She's actually really nice, and she really wants to be your friend," said Cora. "She's been working with her mom to make you a green T-shirt with a nickname on the front. I know you don't like Ronny, so they were trying to think of a new nickname, but to tell you the truth, all the ideas were terrible: Veve and Roro and Nini. Even Caca!"

I snorted with laughter. "That really is a terrible nickname. Camille would agree. Anyway, I don't think I mind Ronny so much. I'm kind of used to it by now."

Cora smiled.

"Do you think..." started Cora. "I mean, do you think we can *all* be friends?"

Three's a Crowd

I was going to say "Yeah, sure," but then I decided to be honest.

"I don't know," I said. "I guess I can give it a try."

"That sounds good to me," said Cora. She boinged a few of her curls. "Sooooooo . . . do you want to open—"

I interrupted her. "Yes! Yes! Yes! Yes! Present, PLEASE!"

I had never seen such a huge shopping bag in my life, and I was really curious about what was inside. I had been sneaking peeks at it out of the corner of my eye, and I could have sworn I saw it move.

Then I heard a sound coming from the bag. It was a rumbling sound, like a little roller coaster.

"Is it a robot?" I guessed. "A set of jumbo-size hair curlers? A time machine?"

Cora laughed. "Just look inside!"

I yanked the sides of the bag down and saw . . .
a cage!

And inside the cage, running on a shiny wheel,
was a tiny little hamster!

"Is it *real*?" I whispered.

Cora giggled. "Of course he is!"

It felt like my heart was jumping for joy on the
biggest trampoline in the world. *Thump! Thump!*
Thump!

I was too happy and excited to talk, so I just
made sounds. "Eeeeeeeee! Yaaaaaaaa! Oooooooh!"

I brought my face right up to the bars of the
cage so I could get a closer look.

The hamster was all light brown, like the color
of a walnut. When he saw me looking at him, he
climbed off the wheel and came sniffing until he
was looking right at me. It was like he knew me!

Three's a Crowd

"Do you like him?" asked Cora.

"Do I *like* him?" I repeated. "I like taking a hot bath on a cold day. I like chocolate-chip cookies fresh out of the oven."

I turned back to the hamster.

"I *love* him!"

But then I remembered something, and my eyes widened.

"But—but I can't keep him!" I said. My voice started to crack. "My dad! He's allergic."

"No, it's all right," said Cora. "My mom asked your parents, and they said it was fine."

"She's right," said Dad, who was standing in the doorway. "I tested it out last week. Apartment 10C has a hamster, and I was there all day installing screens in the windows. No sneezing at all. The hammy can stay."

"Really? Really? REALLY?" I jumped up and threw my arms around Dad, then around Cora.

We looked at each other and then, without saying a word, started to do our secret handshake. I couldn't do most of it because of my cast, and for a second, I felt sad, but then Cora said, "We'll just make up a new one."

So we did. All I can reveal about it is this: There is stuff in that handshake that only we and astronauts can do.

"So what's this little critter's name?" asked Dad.

"That's easy," I said. "Herbert Ewell Conti. Herbie, for short."

It had only been my birthday for an hour or so, but one thing was for sure. Well, two things:

Three's a Crowd

    1. Being eight sure felt great.

and

    2. I was back to being a happy-endings

       sort of girl.

Take the Fix-It Friends Pledge!

I, (say your full name), do solemnly vow to help kids with their problems. I promise to be kind with my words and actions. I will try to help very annoying brothers even though they probably won't ever need help because they're soooooo perfect. Cross my heart, hope to cry, eat a gross old garbage fly.

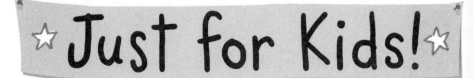

What's in Your Friendship Toolbox?

FIX-IT TOOLBOX

Know that it's not your fault.

Tell your friend how you feel.

Play with other friends.

Talk to a grown-up.

Do stuff that makes you happy.

When Friendships Change . . .

When all's well between you and your bestie, life feels grand. It probably feels like you're skipping together down a smooth path on a sunny day, leaping through rainbows while birds sing sweetly. Ah, friendship! There's nothing better . . .

Until you hit a rough patch. Maybe your best friend's spending lots of time with someone new or just acting differently, but you don't know why, or maybe you're the one who doesn't feel the same way anymore. During these times, you probably feel like you're walking in the pouring rain, on an uneven path, with huge obstacles blocking the way, and your best friend is nowhere in sight. It happens to pretty much all of us. When it does, it's normal to feel upset. It's normal to feel a whole bunch of things.

What did it feel like?

"It feels like you're a mountain and there's two mountains far away from you and the one mountain that is you feels so sad."
—Valentina, age five

"There are three of us, and they are kind of fighting over me. Being caught in the middle is frustrating. I really want them to get along."
—Claire H., age ten

"My friend got a better friend—or that's what I thought. I felt mad and sad and really jealous. I felt all these feelings attacking me, almost."
—Emma, age ten

"My best friend and I met a new friend, and all three of us were hanging out together, but then they started ignoring me. I felt sort of excluded and sad and confused. I thought: 'Why are they doing this?'"
—Claire M., age eleven

"I felt a bit betrayed."
—**Kevin, age ten**

What helped?

"I confronted my friend and gave him a chance to apologize. When he apologized, I felt satisfied, and we became friends again."
—**Finn, age ten**

"Letting the other two cool off after a fight helps a lot. Time makes things better."
—**Claire H., age ten**

"I tried talking to my best friend, but I couldn't find the right moment. I started talking to the people at my table in class, and I made new friends. I still snuck glances at how much fun they were having, but it was much less of a problem."
—**Claire M., age eleven**

> "It helped to play with other friends so I didn't have to feel the empty space between us."
>
> **—Emma, age ten**

What to Do When Friendships Change

What do anacondas, tulips, and friendships all have in common? They're all living things. They start off small, and they grow. And as they grow, they change.

It's not always bad that friendships change. After all, that's what makes it possible for your soccer teammate, who you might barely know, to become one of your closest pals. Of course, when things feel perfect, you want them to stay that way.

When a friendship's changing and you don't want it to, you probably wish you could just make your friend do what you want—hang out with you, treat you nicely, and be happy doing it. The trouble is that you can't control other people—no, not even by hypnosis. No matter how hard you try, it won't work—and it might even make things worse.

But here's the thing: Even though you can't change your friend's feelings or thoughts or actions, you can absolutely change your own. *You* can be okay, even if the friendship's not. Here's how:

1. Know that it's not your fault.

You may wonder if it's your fault that your friend is backing away. You may think, *What did I do? Why don't they want to be my friend anymore?* There are a lot of reasons a friend might want space or to spend time with someone new, but *none* of them is your fault. Don't blame yourself. This is just something that happens.

2. Tell your friend how you feel.

Other people can't read our minds (which is usually a good thing!). Clue them in to how you're feeling but not with accusations like, "You're so mean!" or "You're the worst friend ever!" That'll just make your friend defensive. Instead, start your sentence with "I" and focus on your feelings and not what your friend did. Use phrases like, "I feel left out" or "I want to spend more time with you."

3. Play with other friends.

When it feels like something's slipping away from you, what's your instinct? Grab on tighter, right? Unfortunately, this isn't a good idea when you're dealing with people. The harder you try to get your friend to hang out, be nice, or like you, the more you may push them away. The answer? Reach out to other friends.

Now, you may not want to play with other friends, or you may feel like there's no one else you can play with, but think of it this way: Would you rather sit and stew and feel lousy, or try something a little nerve-racking that will probably be a lot of fun?

Did you choose the second option? Awesome!

Think about kids you talk to a little bit or have played with before. These are the kids you should try first. Or maybe there's an organized activity already set up that you can join. Either way, make a plan beforehand. It's way easier to brainstorm when you're calm. It's not so easy when you're stressed.

4. Talk to a grown-up.

When you're stumped about which other kids to play with, a grown-up can help. When you really want to scream at your friend and call them every name you can think of, talk to a trusted grown-up instead. You don't have to deal with your negative feelings alone—and you shouldn't.

5. Do stuff that makes you happy.

When it comes to being happy, no one knows better than you what will do the trick. Ask yourself, "What can I do to make myself feel better that won't make things worse?" Maybe this means doing something that you already know you love and are great at—like painting or shooting hoops. Maybe this means trying something new that excites you—like rock climbing or learning Portuguese. Maybe it's something special you do with someone you love— like a trip to the trampoline park with your brother or tea with your grandma.

When times are tough with your best friend, it can make you feel alone, but know this: You are not alone. Not by a long shot. There are so many people who care and will help you. And there are so many future friends just waiting to meet you—more than you can even imagine. Cross my heart, hope to sigh, stick my nose in a rotten pie.

Want more tips or fixes for other problems? Just want to check out some Fix-It Friends games and activities? Visit the Fix-It Friends website at fixitfriendsbooks.com!

Resources for Parents

If your child is struggling with friendship troubles, here are some resources that might help.

Books for Kids

A Smart Girl's Guide: Drama, Rumors & Secrets: Staying True to Yourself in Changing Times by Nancy Holyoke, American Girl, 2015

A Smart Girl's Guide: Friendship Troubles: Dealing with Fights, Being Left Out, and the Whole Popularity Thing by Patti Kelley Criswell, American Girl, 2013

Friends: Making Them & Keeping Them by Patti Kelley Criswell, American Girl, 2015

Speak Up and Get Along!: Learn the Mighty Might, Thought Chop, and More Tools to Make Friends, Stop Teasing, and Feel Good About Yourself by Scott Cooper, Free Spirit Publishing, 2005

Books for Parents

Best Friends Forever: Surviving a Breakup with Your Best Friend by Irene S. Levine, PhD, Overlook Press, 2009

Little Girls Can Be Mean: Four Steps to Bully-Proof Girls in the Early Grades by Michelle Anthony, MA, PhD; and Reyna Lindert, PhD, St. Martin's Griffin, 2010

Masterminds and Wingmen: Helping Our Boys Cope with Schoolyard Power, Locker-Room Tests, Girlfriends, and the New Rules of Boy World by Rosalind Wiseman, Harmony, 2013

Odd Girl Out: The Hidden Culture of Aggression in Girls, revised and updated edition, by Rachel Simmons, Mariner Books, 2011

Queen Bees and Wannabes: Helping Your Daughter Survive Cliques, Gossip, Boys, and the New Realities of Girl World, third edition, by Rosalind Wiseman, Harmony, 2016

Websites

The Child Mind Institute

www.childmind.org

The Family Coach

www.thefamilycoach.com

NYU Child Study Center

www.aboutourkids.org

Don't miss the
other adventures of
The Fix-It Friends

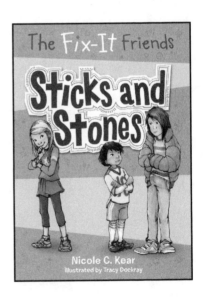

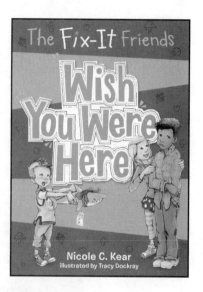

About the Author

Nicole C. Kear grew up in New York City, where she still lives with her husband, three firecracker kids, and a ridiculously fluffy hamster. She's written lots of essays and a memoir, *Now I See You*, for grown-ups, and she's thrilled to be writing for kids, who make her think hard and laugh harder. She has a bunch of fancy, boring diplomas and one red clown nose from circus school. Seriously.

nicolekear.com